Sparkly New Friends

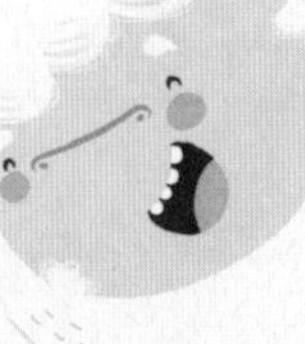

Read more UNICORN and YETI books!

UNICORN and YETI

Sparkly New Friends

written by
Heather Ayris Burnell

art by
Hazel Quintanilla

ACORN™
SCHOLASTIC INC.

For Ellamae, who has always been an amazing friend — HAB

To my brother and sister, my Yeti and Unicorn from real life — HQ

Library of Congress Cataloging-in-Publication Data

Names: Burnell, Heather Ayris, author. | Quintanilla, Hazel, 1982- illustrator.
Title: Sparkly new friends / by Heather Ayris Burnell ; illustrated by Hazel Quintanilla.
Description: First edition. | New York, NY : Acorn/Scholastic Inc., 2019. |
Series: Unicorn and Yeti ; 1 | Summary: Unicorn and Yeti run into each other (literally) while looking for sparkly things, and despite some differences, (for instance Unicorn is magic, Yeti is not, Yeti likes snowball fights, Unicorn cannot throw snowballs)—the two become friends.
Identifiers: LCCN 2018035380 | ISBN 9781338329018 (pbk.) | ISBN 9781338329025 (hardcover)
Subjects: LCSH: Unicorns—Juvenile fiction. | Yeti—Juvenile fiction. | Friendship--Juvenile fiction. | Humorous stories. | CYAC: Unicorns—Fiction. | Yeti—Fiction. | Friendship—Fiction. | Humorous stories. | LCGFT: Humorous fiction.
Classification: LCC PZ7.B92855 Sp 2019 | DDC [E]—dc23 LC record available at http://catalog.loc.gov

10 9 8 7 6 5 4 3 2 1 19 20 21 22 23

Printed in China 62

First edition, May 2019

Edited by Katie Carella
Book design by Sarah Dvojack

Table of Contents

Something Sparkly

Unicorn saw something sparkly.

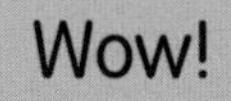

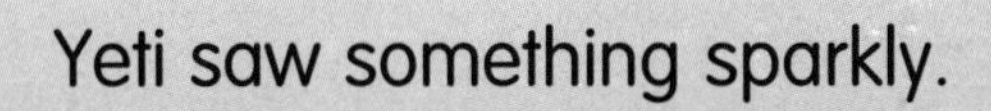

Yeti saw something sparkly.

Wow!

I am going down there.

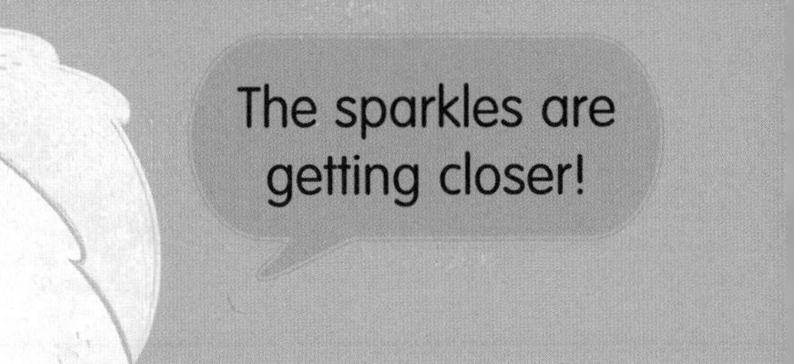

And closer.

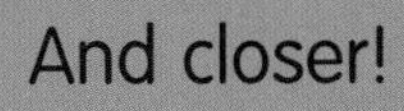

I saw you.
You are the sparkles.

I am very sparkly.

You are lucky.
I wish I had sparkles.

You live in the
most sparkly place
I have ever seen!

There are no sparkles
where I live. It is
white here.

There are **lots** of
sparkles here!

There is snow here.
That is all.

Snow is sparkly.

Snow does not sparkle. Snow is just cold.

Hold the snow up to the light.

This snow does not hold up. It is too fluffy.

What does light have to do with sparkles anyway?

The light is what shows the sparkles.

You are trying to trick me,
because you are so sparkly.

You are a tricky, sparkly horse
with a horn on your head.

I am tricky, and also sparkly. But I am not a horse.
So you **are** trying to trick me.

I am **trying** to show you the sparkles!
There are no sparkles here except for you.
Fine.

Are you going to leave now?
I will miss your sparkles.

Come on.
I will show you
the sparkles.

Unicorn and Yeti flew up . . .

and up . . .

and down.

But mostly up.

The sun is very bright up here.

Look down!

It **is** sparkly where I live!

I told you.

You are tricky.
Thank you.
And you are sparkly.
We already talked about that.
Are you sure you are not a horse?
I am sure.

An Amazing Friend

Unicorn, why do you have
a horn on your head?

I do not know.
I was just born
this way.

Ouch!

Sorry.
I did not see you.
I was looking at
the sparkles.

Yeti, why are you big and furry?

I do not know.
I was just born
this way.

What do you do with your horn?

Lots of things.

Your horn makes you look fancy.
I just look big and furry.

Being big and furry is the best!
It makes you the perfect friend
to have in a snowstorm.

It does not
make me fancy.
I want to be **fancy**.

You could brush your fur.
That might help you look fancy.

I **do** brush my fur.

Okay, I do not brush my fur very much.

I have an idea! I can use magic to make you fancy.

I can make your fur smooth.
Too sleek!
I can make your fur curly.
Too big!

I can make your fur rainbow.

Too colorful!

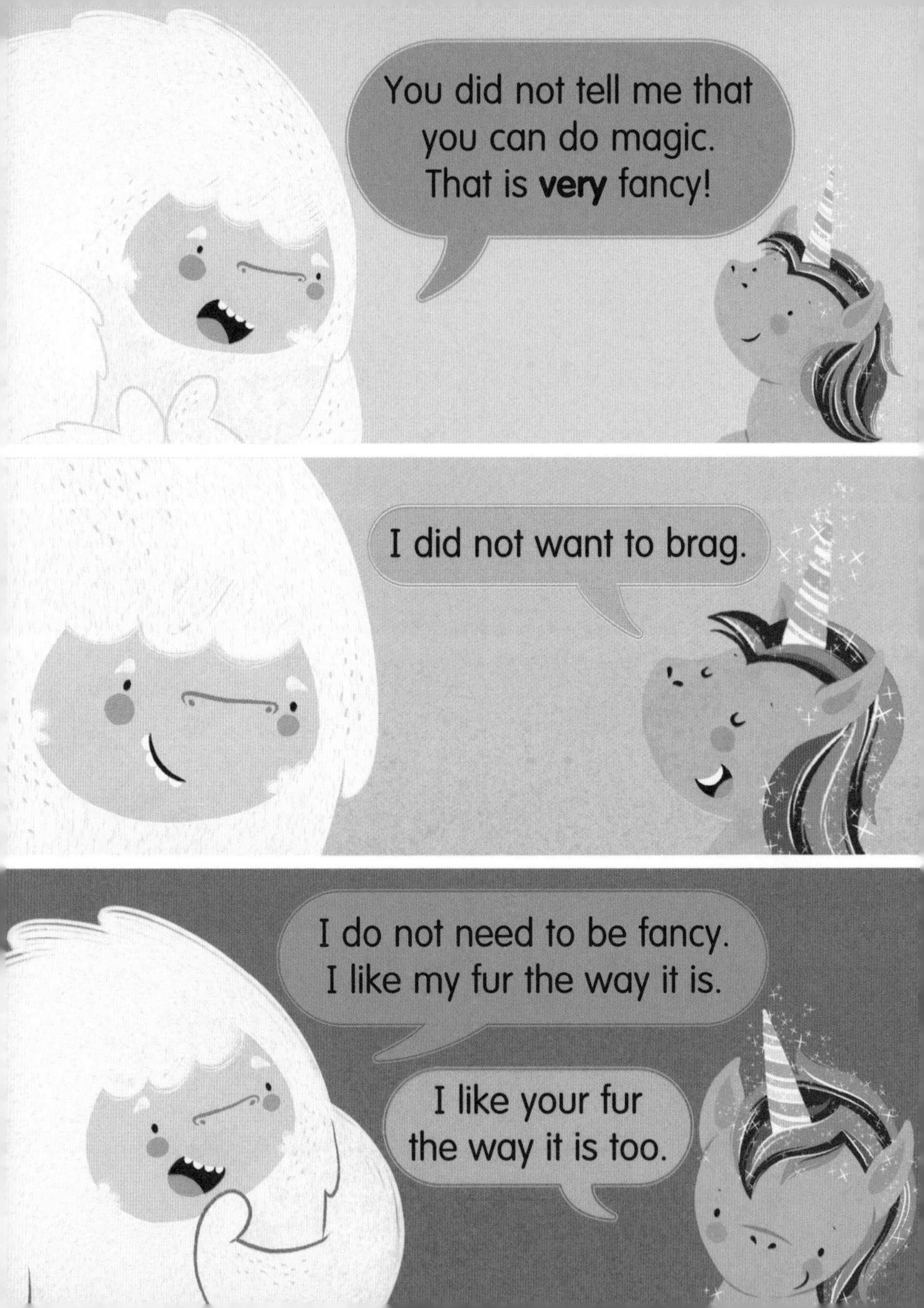

You did not tell me that
you can do magic.
That is **very** fancy!

I did not want to brag.

I do not need to be fancy.
I like my fur the way it is.

I like your fur
the way it is too.

You are an amazing friend.
I would like you even if you
could not do magic.

I know. You did not know I could
do magic until I just showed you.
And we were already friends.

Friends don't need magic
to like each other.

No, they
do not!

But maybe you could
make me something to wear
when I want to be fancy.

A hat would
make me look
fancy.

Yes it would.
I will make you a
super fancy hat!

Now I look fancy!
You sure do!

Snowball Fight

Splat!

Did you **throw** that at me?
I thought we were friends.

It was just a snowball.

Throwing things at your friends
is not nice.

But throwing snowballs is fun.

We could have a snowball fight!

Friends should not fight.
Friends should talk about
their problems.

But we don't have any problems. Do we?

No. A snowball fight
is not a **real** fight.

So you want to have a **pretend** fight with balls of snow?

Yes. But I will probably win. I am very good at snowball fights.

How does a snowball fight work?

First you make a big pile of snowballs.

Making snowballs is hard.

Next you build a fort to protect yourself.

Building a fort is hard.

Then you throw the snowballs!
Oh!

Throw snowballs at me!
I am trying.
Protect yourself in your fort!
My fort is a flop.

You can do it!

I am cold.
I cannot feel my hooves.

Maybe throwing snowballs
is not so easy when
you have hooves
instead of hands.

It is not easy.

I still think you can do it.
Want to try again?

I will do it my
own way!

Splat!
I've been hit!

Snowball fighting is fun
when you splat someone!

Splat!
Splat!
Splat!
I am so snowy!
Splat!
Splat!
Splat!

You are good at snowball fights.

I did not know that I would be good at snowball fights.

I also did not know that friends could fight and still be friends!

Of course they can.

Let's go warm up.
We can have
some soup!

That's a great idea!

You knew just what I needed.

Friends know stuff like that.

Yes! They do.

About the Creators

Heather Ayris Burnell lives in Washington state where she loves spending time in the sparkly snow. Sometimes she even has snowball fights with her friends! Heather is a librarian and the author of *Kick! Jump! Chop! The Adventures of the Ninjabread Man.* Unicorn and Yeti is her first early reader series.

Hazel Quintanilla lives in Guatemala. Hazel always knew she wanted to be an artist. When she was a kid, she carried a pencil and a notebook everywhere.

Hazel illustrates children's books, magazines, and games! And she has a secret: Unicorn and Yeti remind Hazel of her sister and brother. Her siblings are silly, funny, and quirky — just like Unicorn and Yeti!

WHAT'S YOUR STORY?

Yeti wants to be fancy so Unicorn makes him a fancy hat.
What fancy thing would **you** make for Yeti?
What would Yeti do while wearing it?
Write and draw your story!

scholastic.com/acorn